On Reflection

Selected publications

Springtime in the Rockies, poetry

Eight Poems to Photographs of Les Krims, prose-poems

Excursions in the Dark, short fiction

Blocks of Consciousness and the Unbroken Continuum (Ed.), music criticism

Apropos Jimmy Inkling, a novel

The Shenanigans, short fiction

On Reflection

Brian Marley

Published by
grand**IOTA**

2 Shoreline, St Margaret's Rd, St Leonards TN37 6FB
&
37 Downsway, North Woodingdean, Brighton BN2 6BD

www.grandiota.co.uk

First edition 2024

Typesetting & book design by Reality Street

A catalogue record for this book is available from the British Library

ISBN: 978-1-874400-91-2

Even mice sometimes prefer a fictitious reality to the real-life reality.

– *Werner Herzog* –

1.

Catching sight of himself makes him feel physically ill, so he takes pains to avoid mirrors. But despite his best efforts he sees himself everywhere he looks.

Over the years he's devised strategies to avoid his reflection, including the use of modified horse blinkers. Yes, horse blinkers. I know, I know; but in the small equestrian town in which he lived it made him less of a laughing stock than you'd think.

Since moving to the city he wears spectacles with opaque lenses. He tells everyone he's a former racehorse jockey, blinded by a laser-wielding love rival, and that although the gold-digger girlfriend left him toot-sweet for his assailant (the heir to a dot-com fortune and ever so flash with Daddy's cash), he's not bitter, not at all. Yet when they died in a motorway pile-up he reached, by his own reckoning, peak schadenfreude.

Anyway, he simply *loves* being blind. "One could say," he said, "if one felt so inclined, that it's been the making of me."

Leaving the listener agog, he sets off briskly. Visual impairment seems to hamper him not at all. Slim white cane in hand, he powers through the crowd, sweeping the pavement in short, aggressive arcs, scattering pedestrians like skittles in his wake.

2.

Admittedly he's not young any more, but arthritic twinges and toenails so thick they have to be trimmed with bolt cutters make him feel jaded and somewhat older than his years. If only they were all he had to contend with. Various diseases are jockeying for pole position, to see which of them will have the privilege of finishing him off.

It's a race to the death, and although competition is fierce, a cancer of some kind is bound to win, one of the swift ones that don't declare themselves until it's too late.

As everyone knows, the speed at which cancer cells replicate and metastasize leaves the competition – the slow, steady debilitators such as multiple sclerosis, diabetes, Alzheimer's, and a slew of others – aggrieved. But why? This has been going on for millions of years, since the first primitive humans got up on their hind legs and tottered out of what's become known as Africa, so surely they'd be used to it by now.

You'd think so, wouldn't you.

You really would.

Diseases have *feelings* – are you kidding me?

3.

He's in two minds about the Oxford comma and almost everything else, if you must know. And I suppose you must. Sheer curiosity. It's human nature to want to know at least something about everything – a goal that hasn't been achievable since Dante's time. There's too much to know and even the longest life is too short. And some knowledge is of lesser importance anyway.

For example, one of the trees in the background is made entirely of plastic. Yes, plastic. Is there value in knowing whether, in this coastal region of salt breeze and storm spray, it will out-survive the other tree, the woody one?

Does it matter that both trees will probably out-survive him?

About this he's in two minds, as always.

Friends help out as best they can. To put his minds at rest they tell him whatever it is he wants to know, if they know something about it, the thing in question, but sometimes they just make stuff up.

"We were men once," quoth Dante, "though we've become trees."

Plastic or wood – does it really matter?

About this he's also in two minds.

4.

There are those – principally songwriters, reason unknown – who argue that the straitjacket, a crude form of physical restraint, is still widely used in modern-day Italy but, and here's the twist, in the sinister guise of fashion.

He tries the notion on for size. Hmm. An awkward fit, as one might expect. Whereas the jacket on display looks tailor-made for him.

Does he covet it? He does. O how he does! But the store has closed for the day and tomorrow he's scheduled to board his plane hours before opening time.

He wonders who will buy the jacket in his stead and whether the purchaser, a songwriter, because it's obviously a songwriters' jacket (you can tell at a glance), will leave the store with a revolutionary tune pounding in his head, giving him a terrible headache, a banal tune with rabble-rousing lyrics, also banal, composed on the spot to suit the occasion, in which blame is apportioned for his headache, the unaffordably high price of Italian fashion, and much else besides. Heads will roll, come the day, is the gist of it. Of the chorus, at least. The verses bear other grievances, no end of them.

But perhaps, instead of buying the jacket, the songwriter will do what his heroes Phil Ochs and Bob Dylan would have done, might have done, at a push, in a blind panic, back in the day, if sufficiently desperate and, perhaps, drunk – steal it. Immediately his song strikes a triumphal note hitherto undreamt of. The revolution is imminent and the jacket, strait or not, shall be his!

Of the man on the plane we have nothing more to say, other than surely, even with a mind as vacuous as his, he must have better things to think about.

Blauer

5.

Then he remembers: it snowed heavily that year. Winter 1994. The entire country ground to a halt and a man died when an icicle longer than his body broke off from a gargoyle's chin, high overhead, and pierced his skull.

That night he dreamt that's who he was, the UK's sole 1994 icicle victim, until a shift occurred in the dreamscape.

Suddenly he was the man responsible for the maintenance of the cathedral's grotesques and chimeras, contractually bound to carry out emergency repairs whatever the weather. No health and safety legislation worth speaking of back then. No safety harness. Not even gloves. And to his dismay he finds he's wearing inappropriate footwear – flip-flops, the pair he bought in Tenerife last summer.

In conditions that even Ernest Shackleton would have found challenging, he stumbles about in the gutters, and of course he slips (as one does in dreams) and dangles over the precipice (if one can call it that), holding onto a gargoyle with numb fingers that are gradually losing their grip (as they do, with weary familiarity). Yet try as he may he can't recall having fallen.

Perhaps, three decades later, he's dangling there still, icy-fingered, awaiting the resumption of the dream and its tragic denouement.

PUSH

6.

Clockface – the nickname they gave him at school. Since then, and perhaps because of that, his timekeeping has been erratic. He even turned up at the registry office a day late for his wedding, which is why he's still single and probably always will be.

Ah, so what! The true love of his life isn't a person anyway, it's small ceramic figurines. He's been collecting them since childhood. The first one was bought ostensibly for his mother, but he didn't manage to give it to her until a week after her birthday. Near enough, I suppose, his timekeeping being as bad as it was and, just for the record, is. She feigned delight, as mothers do.

The figurine was that of Mother Teresa of Calcutta. Bent in prayer, the nun was shedding tears over a woman dying on a street corner. When his mother passed away he inherited Teresa and dozens of other figurines, all of which he'd bought for her.

In recent years people have been saying nasty things about Teresa, but he won't have it. You don't get to be a saint unless you've done good deeds galore and performed at least one bona fide miracle!

His would-be spouse, a lapsed Catholic, took a fierce dislike to her. "Those are crocodile tears," she hissed, "and that woman is a Janus-faced gila monster or worse!"

From the outset it was obvious their relationship was doomed, but arriving late at the registry office was the final straw. "The way you're going, you'll be dead at least a fortnight before you realise it!" she said. Her parting shot, which struck home, causing major anxiety.

Since then, every time he wakes up he wonders whether he's alive or dead.
Hard to tell, really, all things considered.

SELECTION INSIDE

7.

What if every photo of him were to be destroyed simultaneously by some, I don't know, some kind of image virus, a highly selective photophage that targeted him and him alone, and only, by some freakish circumstance, this self-portrait survived ... And then, worse luck, having just taken the pic, he suffered a devastating insult to the brain ...

That's when all thought in this little thought experiment ran out – or, if you're a rail enthusiast, "hit the buffers".

Perhaps it would have been better to say that just minutes after taking this pic he died in a train crash. Rail enthusiasts would probably perk up at that outcome, though I gather it's unwise to try to second-guess your readers because you're bound to get it wrong. You may even alienate an entirely different niche set of readers.

Assuming, of course, that one has readers. No one seems to read anything nowadays apart from the briefest posts in their Twitter feed and occasionally, among the literati, haiku. Given which, this little thought experiment, with its abrupt lurch into railwaydom, is unlikely to hold the general reader's attention. Fidgety things, readers, especially the general ones.

Ah, but the railway buffs will probably stick around, hoping to hear more about the crash: locomotive type, plate number, etc. The ghoulish ones will also want to know how many people died and what kinds of life-changing injuries the survivors sustained. Model rail enthusiasts will try to glean sufficiently detailed info to enable them to recreate the wreck in their man caves.

I suspect none of them will give even a moment's thought to the man whose unrepresentative self-portrait is the sole visual proof that he ever existed.

That I find terribly poignant, even if you don't.

8.

When Luigi Ghirri walked in, Lee Friedlander jumped to his feet. "Luigi," he cried, bear-hugging him, "so glad you could make it! Let me introduce everyone. This is Arthur Tress, and the fellow by the window, reading Cavafy for the umpteenth time, the smutty bits in particular (if there are any – never read him myself), is Duane Michaels. The joker under the table is Leslie Krims. He's photographing our ankles, don't ask why.

"As I may have mentioned, the person documenting our historic meeting at this quintessential English eatery is ... ah, you already know each other. Excellent! Martin will capture our goofier moments. Some awkward ones too, he's good at that.

"Now sit, sit. Mrs Cunningham is preparing tea and cakes. Even as we speak she'll be making a few well-composed medium-format images of them prior to wheeling them out to us.

"And look, I've brought along a copy of the Zone System. Let's all place a hand on it, layer-cake style, and pledge allegiance to ... heck, I don't know what. Whatever we shutterbugs have most in common. Then we'll toast its author with what Martin would call, in Brit-speak, 'a libation of tea' – right, Martin? – though a slug of bourbon would probably be more appropriate. But as Mrs C. says, 'This parlour isn't licensed for alcohol. *No alcohol to be consumed on the premises.* That's the rule,' says she. And those of you who know her know she's a stickler for the rules.

"Ah, but rules are meant to be broken, and where breakages occur that's where you'll find us, capturing them for posterity, as Martin undoubtedly will. So pass this hip flask around and take a nip. Me first, though, if you don't mind. As the old buckaroo sang in some horse opera or other, 'I'm so goldurned dry I cain't even cry.' *Alla nostra salute!* Knock it back, boys."

Tea Parlour

9.

Hiding behind a pillar is typical behaviour for a shy person, as, being shy himself, he's well aware.

The yellow cone gives fair warning that the person hiding close by should be approached warily, if indeed at all. Shy people sometimes bite if they feel trapped or threatened, and even if you manage to prise their jaws apart (use a crowbar, a fishing rod, a curtain rail, whatever comes to hand) the venom in their saliva, though rarely fatal, may cause necrosis and even, in extreme cases, limb loss.

If bitten seek medical help immediately. That's the advice given on the few photography courses promoting health and safety among the f-stops. People don't realise that photography is an extremely hazardous occupation, and not just in war zones.

Meanwhile, out at sea, someone is drowning, and someone, probably the same person but possibly someone else, is to blame.

Our photographer wishes to apologise for the fact that due to a technical hitch and adverse light conditions, none of the aforementioned individuals can be seen in this photograph.

It's one of *those* days. Things aren't going terribly well.

He realises he's forgotten to pack the anti-venom that photographers are advised to carry at all times. Shy pre-schoolers are notorious biters and scratchers, their parents usually less so, but it's amazing how quickly a photoshoot can turn ugly.

Is someone hiding behind the pillar? Half an hour has passed and no one has emerged. Typical shy person behaviour. But this I guarantee: trouble always finds a way – to him in particular. Dents in his camera show he's had to use it to fend off attackers on many previous occasions.

10.

What seems to have been captured here is an earth tremor, one of greater magnitude than England usually experiences. Not that the human element can be discounted entirely; that's where most problems occur, especially with the subject in question.

He recalls that his stomach began to rumble as he took the picture. Or perhaps the rumble came from deep in his bowels. Does it matter which? More importantly, would he be deemed responsible if roof tiles came crashing down around him and the pavement shivered and buckled; if gas pipes and water mains ruptured; if street lamps fell, crushing vehicles and injuring pedestrians?

To claim responsibility for an earthquake emanating from bowel or belly would suggest that he thinks he has godlike powers, which of course he hasn't. Luckily, the earthquake, if that's what it was, seems to have resulted in neither damage nor death, not even of mice, though they're sensitive creatures whose hearts are easily broken.

But the following day he reads about an attempt on the world record for domino toppling. Apparently, moments after the last few tiles of the 4,49, 864 had been carefully set in place and the firebreaks had been removed, there was, the organisers say, an ominous rumble, something like an overladen heavy goods vehicle with a knackered gearbox grinding past the venue where the attempt on the record was about to take place, just a few yards from where our subject was snapping this pic, and the first tile wobbled and crashed into the second one, toppling it, and there was nothing the organisers could do but watch in dismay as for the best part of an hour four-million-plus dominoes fell in clattery sequence.

You'd think only a fool would want to claim responsibility for something like that, and you'd be right, but this is not about you.

11.

While taking this photo our subject's mind was elsewhere, as often it is. You can tell by his somewhat dazed expression that he was thinking about the brilliant German engineer Felix Wankel, inventor of the rotary engine and an unrepentant anti-Semite. Throughout the 1930s, Wankel was a member of various National Socialist parties, one of which he founded, and by the early 1940s he was an obersturmbannführer in the SS. Post-war his reputation remained unsullied, at least among petrolheads, especially Nazi petrolheads, many of whom revere him to this day.

Why dazed? In a bay on the parking garage's upper floor our subject had chanced upon a rare Mazda RX-8, the Nemesis, only 72 of which are still in existence. Perhaps he should have taken a photograph of the car rather than of himself, but somehow he didn't.

Critics say that although the Nemesis boasted a state-of-the-art Wankel engine, it had a significant design flaw: blue smoke and fire-cracker farts erupted periodically from its tailpipe. When the actor Patrick Dempsey tootled around Los Angeles in one, people kept diving to the sidewalk thinking a drive-by shooting was taking place.

Decades earlier, Wankel had approached Richard Strauss, hoping to persuade him to finance one of his prototypes. He'd brought along a demonstration model of the engine, half-size, made entirely of wood. Strauss, perhaps to avoid the subject of money, expounded at length on Wagner's musical legacy and the magical properties of the alloy that made Siegmund's sword Notung so powerful. "Build an engine out of that," he said, "rather than wood and you'll sit among the gods at Wagner's right hand."

Bemused, Wankel reinserted the engine into the wooden car he'd made specially for it, hitched the car to a biddable bay and trotted back to Heidelberg.

TO BREAK IN CASE OF FIRE
ROMPERE IN CASO D'INCENDIO
SAFE CRASH®

12.

The piano is plagued by mice. Traps and poisoned bait have failed to eradicate them. They scorn the bait and trigger the traps without doing themselves harm, just to mock the caretaker, or so it seems. Whatever their intention, he takes it personally.

They pluck the piano strings with their paws and stroke them with their tails, making a music that's initially beguiling but eventually naught but annoying. Although the caretaker comes from a musical family, he hasn't a musical bone in his body. He can't even keep a steady rhythm on the triangle.

His big brother, the conductor of the Berlin Philharmonic, consults with his big sister, the internationally renowned cellist, about their baby brother's problem. Problems, rather; this being but one of many. They introduce him to a specialist piano tuner who also happens to be the world's leading expert in musical instrument pest control. The tuner says he'll tune the piano in a way known only to him, rendering the music the mice make unpalatable to them, occasioning a swift mass exit to a more harmonious realm. That's the theory anyway.

In practice: nuh-uh. Desperate now, the caretaker removes the piano's innards – strings, soundboard, the lot. When that doesn't work, he jimmies out the keyboard, one ivory key at a time, high notes to low, and locks the fall board – and still the mice make music. But how? They have no means of doing so. Yet there it is, mouse music, shimmering in the aether. Now they're even singing, their small, slightly shrill voices piping up as one.

When his employers discover what he's done, they'll fire him, no doubt about it. He sits, staring at the piano, brooding. Then he climbs up on the fall board, lifts the case lid and leaps into the housing. He's jammed tight, can't move, can't breathe. The mice play around his feet and sing, and he thinks that perhaps, if only he could breathe, he'd sing too, mocking himself to death, the death he so richly deserves.

13.

His annoying friend in the jaunty green trilby is always so sure of himself, even, perhaps especially, when he's wrong, as more often than not he is. "They say every man should have a hobby," his friend declares. "But staring into the void? C'mon, that's a vocation, surely."

Because he's a little deaf he mishears "vocation" as "vacation", which sets off a train of thought about a trip taken, at his friend's behest and against his better judgement, to the site of the Bergen-Belsen concentration camp. This makes him feel queasy, as it did then.

Which in turn reminds him of summer 1963, when he stayed at a camp of a different sort on England's North Sea coast. His parents had paid for a friend – yes, the same one – to accompany him on holiday. The main recollection he has of it is a screening of the James Bond film *Dr No,* in which 007, while imprisoned in a squalid cell by the arch villain, flicks a tarantula off his shoulder and pounds it to death with the heel of his shoe, a moment of high tension undercut by the drunken wag in the audience who yelled "Butlin's!"

It would probably be best if he cut his friend loose and they went their separate ways. What kind of friend is he anyway, apart from annoying, and what kind of question is that? In both cases: the pointless kind. But he knows he'll do no such thing.

He's unaware that his friend feels boundless fraternal love for him and has used a small legacy to buy twin graveyard plots. He – the friend – wants them to lie side by side for all eternity, or at least until the graveyard is torn up to make way for a development of so-called executive homes that will, no matter how well heated they are and how lavishly furnished, possess the cold, dark ambience of tombs.

"All in all, the void is best avoided," his annoying friend says, "if one can."

Unfortunately, he's not sure he can.

14.

Things in this photograph that can't be seen with the naked eye:

- Cufflinks, unostentatious, in each of which a tiny glass phial of cyanide is stored. WW2 issue. German military. The liquid cyanide has long since turned to dust and may now be harmless, but who shall he test it on to find out whether that's the case – a friend, relative, or perhaps, to avoid police scrutiny, a stranger?
- £600 in unmarked twenties, a debt repaid in full. Part of the proceeds from a robbery carried out by his brother, a crime of which our subject is blissfully unaware but to which, because his bro has moved in with him and therefore, inadvertently, he's harbouring a fugitive, he's perhaps become an accessory after the fact.
- A veritable honker of a prosthetic nose, modelled on that of comedian James Francis Durante, aka The Schnoz. Designed to be worn, as it were, over-nose, which it can be because our subject's nose is little more than a cuff button among button noses.
- A pacemaker from the Kappa 400 series. No longer a leading model but that's irrelevant. Kept for juju purposes only, to ward off the demon responsible for cardiac arrest and, coincidentally, muggings.
- The so-called secret recipe for Coca-Cola, found among the notebooks of Charles le Sorcier, an actual person used as a character by H.P. Lovecraft in his juvenile story "The Alchemist". Its original use: cleaning candelabras and sconces.
- A black tie, rolled. Emergency funeral wear. Though never used for that purpose, it once served as a tourniquet when a hedge trimmer dug a crevasse in one of his neighbour's meaty thighs. Because of our subject's decisive action, both the neighbour and his leg were saved ... so he tells everyone, even strangers on trains, most of whom, the sensible ones, quickly shy away.

BEAUFOY & Co's
PURE MALT
Vinegar
GUARANTEED BREWED from FINEST MALT
South Lambeth, LONDON, S.W.

15.

Having muffed the sawn-in-half-but-miraculously-whole routine at the Hackney Empire, he knew his career as a stage magician's "handsome assistant" was over. He'd always been a bit cack-handed but of late he'd got worse. What transpired was worse still: for ruining her act and a thousand other sins, his magician-wife filed for divorce.

As for remaining in showbiz in some other capacity, after the Hackney debacle that proved impossible. Offers of stage work dried up immediately, and by the time of the *decree nisi* he couldn't even get a job as a scene-shifter at a third-rate provincial theatre.

Months later, when the *decree absolute* finalised the divorce, it was winter, bitterly cold, and he was homeless, sleeping rough in shop doorways, his clothes padded out for warmth with copies of *The Stage*.

It's in the blood, they say, thespianism and all things theatrical; also, in his case, a subspecies of the bacterium *treponema pallidum*. Devastating brainstorms may ensue in the tertiary phase of the infection, resulting in delirium, hallucinations and jerky movements. Hence, I suppose, his odd behaviour and awkwardness. Though perhaps the bacterium did nothing more than exacerbate problems he already had. But really, who knows.

The following year his ex-wife, by then a theatrical agent, was fatally stabbed by a ventriloquist whose act was premised on Stan, his dummy, being Satan. A good idea – the premise, I mean. But a series of poor notices and no new bookings enraged him, and his claim in court that it was Satan/Stan who struck the fatal blow fared no better than his act.

Apportioning blame for personal tragedies such as these is difficult, but whichever way you slice it the Mrs Worthingtons of this world have a hell of a lot to answer for.

MARKS
JEWELLERY & ANTI
WATCHES, BRONZES & DECORATIVE ITEMS

16.

Nothing is quite as it seems, not in our warped corner of the universe. There is, for example, a mistake in this photograph, an error of some kind. Can you spot it?

The dog is missing. A little dog, perhaps a Pomeranian. Yes, that's what's missing, a little dog. Every photograph worth its salt contains a little dog, and as there isn't one here ...

No, try again.

A troupe of acrobats drumming up business for their matinee show by forming a human pyramid out in the street.

No.

A Mayan pyramid? An Egyptian pyramid?

Neither of those.

A spin-dryer as powerful as a tornado that's guaranteed to spin your clothes to Oz and back.

Now you're just being silly.

A pop-up crematorium. Am I getting warmer?

No, and an absence of presence does not in itself constitute an error.

Then I give up.

Bravo! Life holds no greater joy than pointing out other people's mistakes, especially to the mistake-maker. But you've given up on that particular joy, as eventually do we all. Most of us then abandon joy entirely and resign ourselves to our fate. That, my friend, is how the world wags. Your missing dog, perhaps, too.

PLEASE
DO NOT ENTER
dining in elegant, tasteful surroundings...
Far East Menu
CAUTION
WET
FLOOR

17.

He and his reflection aren't as close as they once were. Not only have they become physically less alike, they're gradually drifting apart. Some mornings he can hardly recognise the rumpled, bleary-eyed troll staring back at him in the shaving mirror.

It's natural to assume that his reflection is subordinate to him, because without him it wouldn't exist. But that doesn't appear to be the case.

Apparently, his reflected self has a life of its own, one that until recently he knew nothing about. A friend said, "I saw you yesterday at the shopping centre, photographing, as per, and so deep in concentration I thought it best to leave you be."

Trouble is, he hadn't been anywhere near the centre.

Later that evening he finds images on his camera he's sure he didn't take, hundreds of them, dating back almost a year. The most recent batch chimes with his friend's recollection of time and place. What the hell is going on?

More photos turn up on old memory cards, of intimate evenings spent with people unknown to him, of trips to distant cities he's never visited. In every pic he looks as though he's having fun, more fun than he's ever had or thought possible. His reflection's social life is evidently richer and more fulfilling than his own.

Have he and his reflection somehow changed places? Is he now but a pale reflection of his reflection? If so, he's entered a realm of infinite regress, in which gradually he'll become lost among myriad reflections, unsure which of them is actually him.

But fun ... there'll be more fun.

He's perfectly willing to subordinate himself to that.

18.

In the early hours, before getting up to pee, he dreams he's in hiding from a loan shark enforcer by the name of Spifflicator Jones, the self-styled "neutron bomb in human form". Whereas in actuality he's hiding from Malcolm King, aka Megaton Malky, so-called because his fists cause massive explosions of pain.

Once King has knocked the door off its hinges, he'll demand, with menaces, because he enjoys menaces even more than blunt-trauma mano a mano sex, payment of a vig that's already ten times the principal. Cash our subject doesn't have and can't get, no matter how. He is, as they say, fucked. Or will be. Royally fucked, if you prefer.

It's exhausting to have dreams hew so close to reality that it's all but impossible to tell them apart.

Having drained his bladder, he goes back to bed but can't sleep. Nor would you if you had his problems. But his mind drifts, as minds do, and soon he's dreaming again, this time of Samuel T. Cohen.

When Cohen invented the neutron bomb he called it "the most sane weapon ever devised". Depends on how you define sane, of course.

A destroyer of people and other fleshlings but with a low explosive yield and short half-life, the bomb leaves infrastructure largely intact (see illustration), making a return to "normal life" under the new regime's wicked overlords possible after just a decade or so.

In the post-pee dream he asks Cohen for a loan to get Spifflicator Jones off his back, and to his surprise and considerable relief Cohen, without quibble, agrees. "Sure," he says, "no problemo. After all, I invented Jones, even though he's in your dream."

If only Megaton Malky could be dispatched so easily. If only he could be dreamt away.

CLOSED
PETER TREVOR Jewellers
SHORTCUTS
BARBER SHOP

19.

As our subject was lining up the shot, a passerby called out "Deanna Durbin!" Was he being sarcastic? Not that our subject cares a hoot what anyone thinks of him. Nor, for that matter, of the delectable Miss Durbin, one of the few stars of Hollywood's golden era who looked, as in the famous rhyme, good in a turban.

In her movies, when cast as an unsavoury character, she always came across as a good girl playing bad; an image she carefully cultivated. Too good to be true yet none truer, that was Deanna Durbin.

Having given little or no thought to what might happen at bedtime, when hormones rage, men nonetheless wanted to marry her, and three of them managed to do just that, though the first two proved unsatisfactory and were swiftly dumped.

By comparison, Doris Day, Durbin's rival in perky wholesomeness, inspired deviant cravings and ungovernable lust – according, that is, to Alfred Kinsey's Report, which revealed in detail the disgusting sexual preferences and practices of the average American male.

It's well known that Kinsey was a fan of both Durbin and Day, as was J. Edgar Hoover, but despite having that in common he and Hoover didn't get along. Hoover was furious with Kinsey for refusing to help the FBI identify closeted gays in the U.S. state department, and when he and Kinsey met to discuss the matter, Kinsey avoided shaking his hand.

A wise move, and not just for ethical reasons. Durbin told a friend in strictest confidence that Hoover's hand was cadaver-cool and somewhat slimy. "The hand," as she put it, according to her tittle-tattle friend, "of a chronic self-abuser."

Only Hoover's "secret" boyfriend, Clyde Tolson, would know the truth of that claim, but if Tolson was good at anything he was good at keeping secrets, and that's one he took to his grave.

20.

Self-effacing, that's how he thinks of himself, when he gets round to thinking of himself, which isn't all that often, modesty being one of his defining trai—

Let's stop him right there, shall we? By the powers vested in me, I can do that. His hand is now stilled an inch above the keyboard, fixed in time and space until I decide to release him.

Modest? Hardly. He's a mega-narcissist for whom the selfie is a barely adequate tool of self-expression. Even in a debased society such as ours, in which self is celebrated regardless of merit, he stands head and shoulders above his fellow egomaniacs. But that's not nearly enough, not for him.

He courts security cameras. He won't walk down a suburban street unless he thinks he'll be under surveillance from one house to the next, one end of the street to the other. The route of his thrice-daily constitutionals (for which he's hired a dog, to allay suspicion of loitering with intent to commit a criminal act) takes in as many doorbell cameras as possible, the greatest concentration of which are to be found in wealthy neighbourhoods, where fortress security come as standard.

When not pounding the pavement with his canine hireling, he haunts department stores and shopping centres. Not to shop. He's there to have his image registered simultaneously on as many security cameras as possible, thus confirming his existence, at least for that day.

Conversely, on a day to come (for come it surely will) when his image fails to be registered even once, he'll know that although he's not dead he's ceased to exist, which is a conundrum and, as the cliché-mongers say, "a fate worse than death".

Not that one should feel sorry for him. I would hate to have to live with his level of anxiety, but, let's face it, living with him would be infinitely worse.

21.

The time capsule in buried deep underground, and every day at noon one of its exhibits is selected at random and projected into the street as a hologram. That much is known. To enable me to reveal the unknown you must cross my palm with silver.

Without further ado, then ... Occasionally, a glitch in the software traps a pedestrian and drags him down into the capsule, while above ground his simulacrum (if that's what it is) goes about its business as though nothing untoward has happened.

When the capsule is dug up, it will be found to contain skeletal remains, and not just of one or two corpses, no, no – *dozens of them!* The one wearing mayoral robes and a chain of office will be identified as Petal Baltzheim, aka DJ MegaDitz, who served the city to the best of her inability from June 2024 to April 2026.

This grim discovery will trigger speculation that the other skeletons (nearly all men, as it happens) were sacrificial victims, buried with their "queen" to attend her every need in the afterlife.

A ludicrous claim.

As everyone knows, airborne pollution varies markedly from day to day, and analysis of the pollutants on each of the victim's clothes will prove conclusively that they weren't interred at the same time as Baltzheim or indeed with each other.

But a significant legal complication will arise when the bones in the capsule are DNA-matched to bones in the municipal graveyard. Can a person such as your late father (he says "Hi!" by the way) be in two places at once and die twice, his deaths occurring years apart?

The lawyers will rub their hands with glee (whatever that is) when the families of the victims hire them to sue somebody for something or something for something.

Sorry to be so vague. My scrying ball has become a snow globe in storm mode. Only a large quantity of silver crossing my palm will blow that psychic weather bomb away.

22.

When he crossed the road and slipped through the gate, his reflection went with him. So much for the laws of physics or even common sense. But fiction sets its own rules and does what it wants, and what it wants, as always, is to lead you up the garden path.

But is there really a garden behind that gate? Not unless you fancy conjuring one up for yourself. Go ahead, I'm a staunch advocate of the creative reader. While you busy yourself with that, I'll press on. Catch up with me when you can.

Okey-dee, while the "creatives" are gardening to their minds' content, let me take this opportunity to thank you, loyal readers, for sticking with this fiction to the end. I almost said "bitter end" because, sorry to say, your reward will be meagre. Frankly, given how this is shaping up, the conclusion is likely to be a whinge and a bore.

Aha, here they come, the mind gardeners, looking terribly smug. I assume they've skipped the previous paragraph and think this fiction still has legs, sturdy ones at that. But let's hope they don't want to tell me about their imaginary gardens, I'm really not interested. This less-than-exemplary tale, which benefits from brevity if nothing else, is the only thing I'm interested in, though not for much longer.

We only have his word for it that he, the man in the photo, took his reflection with him. I'm simply telling you what he told me, in a pub so dimly lit I could scarcely make him out from across the table, if indeed it was a table. He may not even have been who he said he was and I, deep in my cups, may have misunderstood him.

Yet I'll be dubbed an unreliable narrator and he'll walk away scot-free.

Where, I ask you, is the justice in that?

23.

Here he sees himself as he'd like to be seen, if at all. He craves invisibility, which, as we all know, is unattainable. Nonetheless, because of his longstanding commitment to invisibility, he's been inducted into the Secret Order of the Invisible Man, a society of actors who've played the role on stage and screen, plus a few special others, of which he's one.

He models himself on Vincent Price in *The Invisible Man Returns*, and Price gives him valuable acting tips. He even does a little voice coaching with him. Soon our subject tells him, in eerily Pricean tones of lightly crushed velvet, what led to him joining the Order. A confused tale. Something about the murder of his brother, Michael, for which, though innocent, he'd been found guilty and was due to be hanged. By feigning invisibility he'd managed to escape and ... well, that's where real life and the film script significantly diverge.

Thing is, he *had* murdered his brother, not that he was about to tell Price that, and he craves invisibility because, while on the run, he'd barely managed to keep one step ahead of the law and knew that one day he'd stumble and fall.

The Secret Order HQ is a place of sanctuary, one he daren't leave.

Having assumed the role of janitor, in which Price says he's superb, utterly convincing, a janitor for the ages, he whiles away his remaining years pushin' broom Roger Miller style.

So many holes to this story. Are we to assume, for example, that famous singer Roger Miller is one of the "special others"? If not, where might our subject have learned Miller's unique push-broom technique, as mentioned in the song *King of the Road*, that swung the audition in his favour?

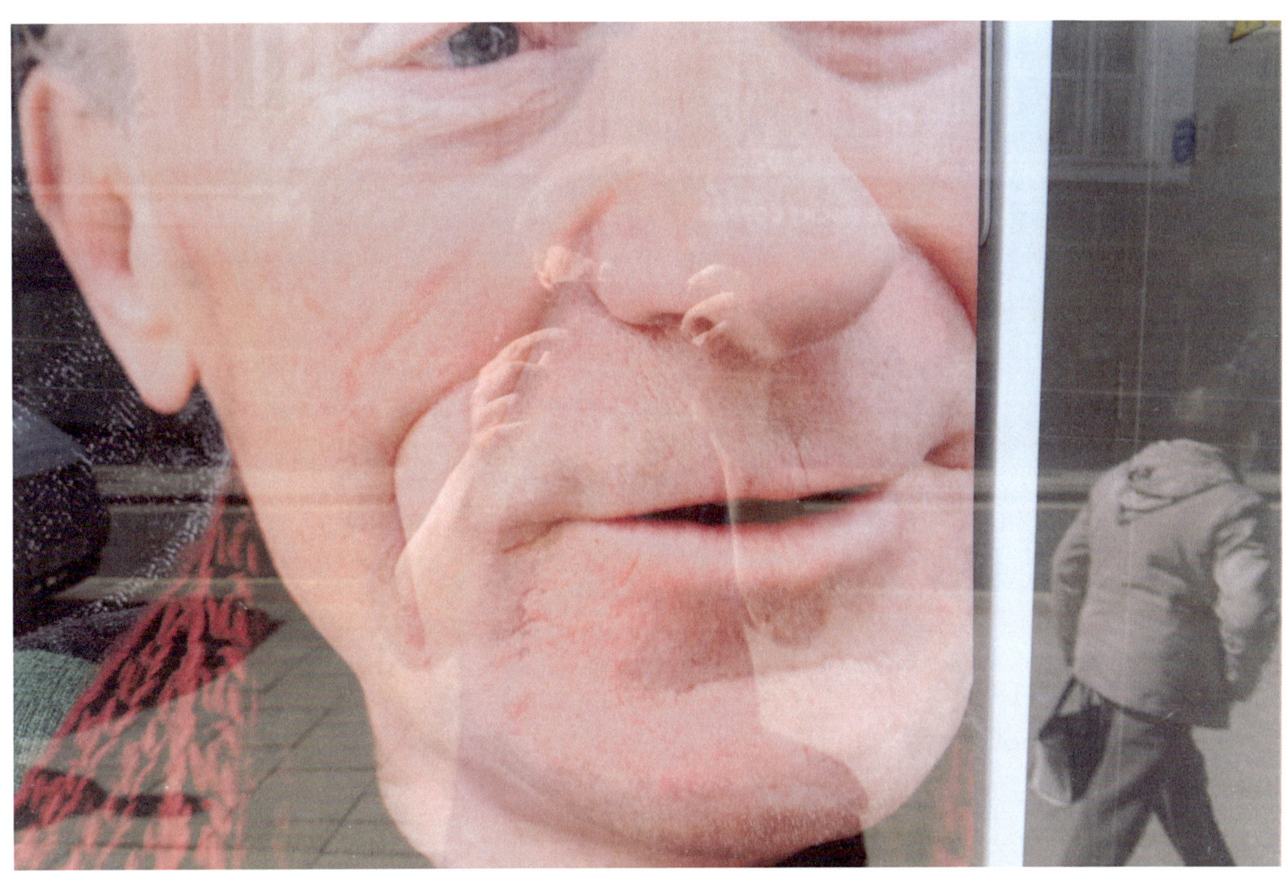

24.

When the aliens land it will look something like this, he thinks. But why are they here and what are their intentions? Two important questions tandemed in a single sentence – good value for money if you're on a tight budget, and, let's face it, who isn't?

"We're here to make your lives better," they'll say, when asked, as they will be on media channels worldwide and in all languages simultaneously. "Nothing would please us more than to greatly increase your quantum of happiness, and that's precisely what we intend to do." But they would say that, wouldn't they? They'd say just about anything to get one over on us. They'll even go so far as to split an infinitive, to show how likeably fallible they are, just plain, ordinary Does – Johns mainly, though a few Janes – little different from you and me.

He knows that despite our apparent scepticism we'll be taken in, as gullible as ever, especially if the aliens, having concluded that money is the surest and swiftest route to happiness, offer us as much of it as we want – which of course they will, they'd be crazy not to, and crazy is what they're not, damn them!

Money's a game-changer. Money decides everything. If the aliens control money then inevitably they'll control us. He wonders whether he should notify the governor of the Bank of England of the coming danger, to give him time to formulate a contingency plan, and perhaps Hollywood could be persuaded to invent an aliens-only death ray, they're good at that kind of thing.

But, a sudden thought: What if the aliens *are* money, then what?

What indeed. This is getting mind-bogglingly complicated. Time for him to take a restorative nap or emerge from the one he's been having for much of his sorry life.

25.

"Death. It's all about death, isn't it?" he says to anyone foolish enough to listen (the fools being few in number nowadays). In years gone by he'd set up his soap box on street corners, megaphoning his death-squawks at distortion level into the still suburban air. Being heckled and pelted with dog muck proved no deterrent to someone as resolute as him. He knows what he knows and he's determined that you should know it too.

For his own safety the police moved him on, but no sooner had they departed than he set up on another corner. Let's face it, there are no end of corners in suburbia, including blind ones that impatient drivers speed around, causing head-on collisions that result in injury and, yes, death. Those were the ones he liked best.

His obsession – that's really not too strong a word – with death quickly became an embarrassment to friends and family. One by one they slipped their moorings and drifted away. In the absence of conversation, his thoughts became ever more single-minded, and he spent much of his time alone, talking to himself. Unsurprisingly, he found he agreed with himself about absolutely everything, which was a comfort.

One day soon, death will vulture down to snatch him away, and you'd think, given the nature of his obsession, he'd welcome it, wouldn't you?

In answer to that question, please tick box **YES** ☐ or box **NO** ☐.

We, the National Association of Funeral Directors, thank you for participating in our survey.

CLOSED

Locations

COVER	Brighton
1.	Rye
2.	Eastbourne
3.	Brighton (Marina)
4.	Bergamo
5.	Shoreham-by-Sea
6.	Seaford
7.	Bergamo
8.	Newcastle-upon-Tyne
9.	Southsea
10.	Seaford
11.	Bergamo
12.	Newcastle-upon-Tyne
13.	Worthing
14.	Lewes
15.	Seaford
16.	Worthing
17.	Newcastle-upon-Tyne
18.	Brighton
19.	Portslade
20.	Brighton
21.	Brighton
22.	Newcastle-upon-Tyne
23.	Worthing
24.	Seaford
25.	Newcastle-upon-Tyne

Also available from grand**IOTA**

Brian Marley: APROPOS JIMMY INKLING
978-1-874400-73-8 318pp

Ken Edwards: WILD METRICS
978-1-874400-74-5 244pp

Fanny Howe: BRONTE WILDE
978-1-874400-75-2 158pp

Ken Edwards: THE GREY AREA
978-1-874400-76-9 328pp

Alan Singer: PLAY, A NOVEL
978-1-874400-77-6 268pp

Brian Marley: THE SHENANIGANS
978-1-874400-78-3 220pp

Barbara Guest: SEEKING AIR
978-1-874400-79-0 218pp

Toby Olson: JOURNEYS ON A DIME
978-1-874400-80-6 300pp

Philip Terry: BONE
978-1-874400-81-3 150pp

James Russell: GREATER LONDON: A NOVEL
978-1-874400-82-2 276pp

Askold Melnyczuk: THE MAN WHO WOULD NOT BOW
978-1-874400-83-7 196pp

Andrew Key: ROSS HALL
978-1-874400-84-4 190pp

Edmond Caldwell: HUMAN WISHES/ENEMY COMBATANT
978-1-874400-85-1 298pp

Ken Edwards: SECRET ORBIT
978-1-874400-86-8 254pp

Giles Goodland: OF DISCOURSE
978-1-874400-87-5 302pp

Rosa Woolf Ainley: THE ALPHABET TAX
978-1-874400-88-2 182pp

John Olson: YOU KNOW THERE'S SOMETHING
978-1-874400-89-9 192pp

James Russell: THE GRIFFIN BRAIN & OTHER STORIES
978-1-874400-90-5 244pp

Production of this book has been made possible with the help of the following individuals and organisations who subscribed in advance:

Rosa Woolf Ainley
Paul Bream
Andrew Brewerton
Ian Brinton
Jasper Brinton
Mark Callan
Allen Fisher
Fred Grand
Leopold Haas
Charles Hadfield
Andrew Hamilton
Randolph Healy
Lindsay Hill
Peter Hodgkiss
Gad Hollander
Kristoffer Jacobson
Elizabeth James
Al Jones
Howard Jones
Richy & Gill Johnson
Nick Lambert
Ian Land
Richard Makin
Paresh Malhotra
Alan Marley
Joe Milazzo
John Olson
Toby Olson
Sean Pemberton
Simon Perril
Dennis Phillips
Margaret Poulton
Lou Rowan
Antony Rudolf
James Russell
Alan Singer
Eileen Tabios
Julian Thomas
Robert Vas Dias
Barrett Warner
Carol Watts
Lillian Michiko Yano

www.grandiota.co.uk

www.ingramcontent.com/pod-product-compliance
Lightning Source LLC
Chambersburg PA
CBRC091355010726
47507CB00006B/271

9781874400912